# Phyllis Clark;
# Sunday Afternoon in the Park



By

## A. P. Dunar

# Chapter One

# Another August Day

The hot, sticky month of August was quickly drawing to an end in Chicago as Phillip Clark opened the connecting door to his granddaughter's office.  He had intended to ask her if she wanted a cup of coffee and a doughnut, but stopped short suddenly when he caught Phyllis and her husband, Benjamin, kissing.  They hadn't realized that he had opened the door, so he quickly and silently pulled it shut again.  He felt badly that he had once again forgotten to knock.  Phillip turned to the door that led out to the common area where the desks of the newer detectives and the waiting area were located, along with the reception desk.  He figured that he was safe taking this route to the coffee and doughnuts.  He was wrong.  As he opened the door he spotted Duck and Jackie kissing at Jackie's desk.  Upon turning quickly away with embarrassment, he found Nora and Patterson kissing at the reception desk.  Taken by surprise, Phillip clumsily tried to duck back into his office, but it was too late.  Jackie and Duck were startled and looked at him, even more embarrassed than he was.

"Sorry, Mr. Clark," moaned Duck with awkward humiliation.

Jackie just blushed and giggled. Nora and Patterson jumped like two kids caught by the usher in the last row of a movie theater.

Phillip felt awkward and smiled, "That's ok. As you were. Apparently that's what we do around here, now."

Jackie chuckled, "Didn't you and Mrs. Clark ever kiss in the office when the two of you were young?"

Phillip didn't sneak back into his office. Instead, he stood there for a moment thinking.

"As I remember, we did plenty of necking, and not just when we were young," Phillip remembered fondly. "But it was mostly at home, or parked in the park. I don't remember doing much of it in public. And I know that we never did any necking here in the office. Back then public displays of affection were frowned on, especially in a professional setting. And for a private eye to be seen kissing…well, it just wasn't right back in them days. It sent the wrong message."

"Sorry, Sir," sighed Jackie. "Mr. and Mrs. Attlee do a lot of kissing."

Phillip chuckled, "Yeah, don't worry about it. Apparently times have changed. I'll just get my Java and a doughnut and go be a dinosaur in my office."

"I made the coffee this morning, Sir," Jackie said happily.

"Thank God," Phillip returned. "You're a lucky man, Duck. Jackie makes a pretty good cup of Joe."

Duck smiled, "That's not all she's good at."

Jackie punched Duck in the shoulder, "Don't you ever think before you talk?"

Duck looked confused, "I was just about to say what a great cook you are."

"Not to mention that she's not a bad detective," added Phillip.

"See, not everyone thinks the way you do," scolded Duck.

"I was thinking the same thing as Jackie," sighed Patterson.

"Of course, you were!" admonished Nora. "That's all you ever think of."

Everyone snickered at Nora's comment as Phillip approached the counter where the coffee and doughnuts were kept.  There, sitting on the counter, were six bottles of Haig Pinch Scotch whiskey.

"What do we have here?" Phillip asked in surprise.  "It seems that Christmas has come early!"

He read the cards that were attached to the bottles.  One pair was for Jackie and Duck, one pair was for Phyllis and Benjamin, and the last pair was for him.  Phillip read the card that was addressed to him.

The card read, "Thank you very much for what you did for my Aunt.  I'm so very sorry for all the trouble that I've been for you.  Deeply in your debt, Doctor Strange."

Phillip smiled and took his two bottles of fine Scotch in his arms like babies.

"You're a good kid, Patterson.  I don't care what anyone says," shouted Phillip as he retreated into his office.  "I'll make sure that these babies are well taken care of."

Patterson and Nora had stopped kissing and were watching Phillip.  They both smiled with satisfaction.

"I told you that the way to his heart was through Scotch," chuckled Duck.

"Thanks, Duck," returned Patterson.

Phillip sat down at his desk, opened one of the bottles of fine scotch whiskey, and poured about two ounces into a water glass. Phillip then leaned back in his high back swivel chair and sipped his present. As he sipped, he considered pursuing an idea that had popped into his head a few minutes earlier. The accountant who maintained the office suite directly next door to Phillip's offices had mentioned that he was about to retire at the end of the year. Phillip suddenly realized that this would give him the opportunity to expand his own offices when the accountant vacated his. Originally he had considered it and quickly rejected the idea, but right now, it seemed like a much better idea. Jackie and Duck could each have their own office and Benjamin could move out of his converted storage room into a real office. Phillip decided to look into it. He sipped some more scotch.

Six and two-thirds miles south of the Uptown Building, at the Chicago Art Institute, a team of men were busy making the last preparations for a very special painting to be loaned to another museum.  The director of the Art Institute was considerably on edge over the transport and loan of this particular work of art.  He had good reason to be.  It was not just another irreplaceable piece of art, but one of the most iconic works of art of all time.  Georges Seurat's, *Sunday Afternoon on the Island of Grand Jatte,* is perhaps one of the most recognizable works of art ever.  It is the epitome of what has come to be known as "pointillism", a form of neo-impressionism painting where millions of tiny dots of paint are arranged on a canvas to form what the human eye perceives as solid forms.

Not only was the fact that this was an important and beautiful painting, valued at the time around $124,500,000.00, but the very museum which was borrowing it had done so seventeen years earlier.  It was the only time in the fifty-one years of ownership that the Chicago Art Institute had ever loaned it out before this time.  What made the director so concerned was the fact that while it had been at the Museum of Modern Art in New York, it had come close to being destroyed.  As it was being displayed on the second floor of the Museum of Modern Art, there was a fire on the floor right beneath it.  Miraculously, even though the fire killed one person, the Seurat painting suffered no harm. However, it had to be moved to the nearby Whitney Museum.

Needless to say, this incident was enough to cause everyone concern. Most on edge over the loan was the company who insured the painting.

The painting had been brought down to the basement from where it was usually displayed right after closing on Tuesday night. Then on Wednesday, a team of restoration and repair people covered it with the fireproof protective wrapping. The director and security chief nervously supervised. The painting was then left in the high security basement Wednesday and Thursday while the carpentry crew custom built a crate for its transport.

"I want to make sure that nothing but inflammable packing materials are used in the transport of this painting," the Director ordered the security chief.

"Even the wood used for the crate has been treated by being soaked in a fire retardant. But at what this baby is worth, I'd be more worried about it getting stolen," moaned the museum's chief of security.

"It's seven feet tall and ten feet wide and weighs over two hundred pounds!" exclaimed the museum director. "And it is one of the most recognized works of art in the world. Who would even attempt to steal it? How on earth would you ever fence a thing like this? You'd be much better off stealing the Hope Diamond. At least you could stick that in your pocket."

The security chief shrugged his shoulders and frowned, "People steal stuff just for the challenge these days."

"Don't even think that," whined the Director. "Don't you know that it's bad luck?"

All the men who were busy getting the painting ready to load onto the truck chuckled and snickered, being careful not to let their boss see them.

Back on the north side, Phillip Clark once again stepped out of his office. He was happy to see that no one was necking in the outer office, although he did wonder what was going on in his granddaughter's office. But then, he didn't really want to know.

"Boyfriend go home?" Phillip asked Nora as he walked toward the outer door.

Nora nodded, "He's picking me up after work."

Phillip nodded, "Let everyone know that I'm off to the Cubs game. They're playing the Atlanta Braves at Wrigley this afternoon."

"It's really cloudy out there. Do you think that it might rain?" wondered Nora.

"With me going to the game it most likely will," snickered Phillip as he left.

"Have fun, Sir," Nora said exuberantly. "And thank you for letting us have the whole week off."

Phillip chuckled, "Duck and Jackie earned the time off and you don't do very much when you are here. I needed the rest anyway."

Nora giggled as Phillip closed the door. It didn't rain and the Cubs actually won, eight to three.

Back downtown, the now wrapped and crated Seurat painting, had been loaded onto a museum truck. The museum director watched as the truck pulled up the ramp from the lower basement loading dock. The heavy roll down door was closed and locked. The heavy iron inner doors were swung shut and locked by the security chief. The chief then set the alarm code for this sector and the two left the loading dock.  The Chief closed, locked, and set the alarm on the door to the dock.  The two men then walked through the workroom where museum employees were busy building new display cases and backboards for the traveling display that was scheduled to open the day after Labor Day.

"Sorry about having you guys work over the Labor Day weekend," the director apologized.

"It's well worth the holiday pay that we'll be making," returned the foreman.

The director chuckled and apologized once again as he and the security chief left the work area into the warehouse part of the subbasement.  The carpenters continued with their work.

The truck containing the almost priceless painting was escorted by museum security for the half mile drive to the Illinois Railroad freight dock, which lay under what is now Millennial Park.  Once at the railroad dock, the museum workers, who rode with the painting, transferred it onto its very own special boxcar. The car was equipped with state of the art fire suppression equipment, a tracking device, and a burglar alarm.  Guards would be riding in a railroad work car just behind the painting's boxcar.  This box car and the Illinois Central work car would first be taken by a single switching engine from the Illinois Rail Road yard over to the Penn Central Rail Road freight yard.  It was only a two and a half mile trip under the downtown area of Chicago's loop, hugging the Chicago River.  But the Insurance Company considered it to be much safer than transporting such precious cargo over the crowded city streets.  Once the special boxcar arrived at the freight yards south of Union Station, it would be integrated into a normal Penn Central freight consist going to New York.  When the two cars arrived in the freight yards across the river from Manhattan, they would be separated from the main train and hauled, underground, through New York's complex network of tunnels, right to the Museum of Modern Art's underground loading dock.  The trip used just one part of the 840 miles of tunnels that run as deep as 500 feet beneath the city.  This was the same tunnel system that once was used to carry Presidents and Generals to stations underneath Manhattan hotels, without anyone ever realizing that they were there.

Once the painting arrived at its destination, the plan was to transport it onto an elevator and bring it up to the basement level of the museum.  There it would be uncrated and then moved to the final location where it would be displayed.

Under the most ideal conditions, this trek could take about sixteen hours.  However, realistically, it would take around twenty-two hours.  However, it had been known to take as much as two weeks!  Everyone concerned earnestly prayed that it would not take anywhere near this long.

As the last Friday of August came to a close and the Labor Day weekend began, Patterson picked up Nora just as promised.  Nora locked up the office and placed a sign on the door stating that the Clark Detective Agency was closed until Tuesday, September 2nd.

# Chapter Two

# Labor Day Weekend

As Patterson drove Nora home to pick up clothes for their week of sailing together, Phyllis and Benjamin were on their way to Gulliver's for pizza.

"You know, when I was a kid, the Labor Day weekend was a big thing for my family," sighed Benjamin. "We always did something together."

Phyllis nodded, "We always went to Wisconsin with the O'Malleys."

"Isn't that what they're doing this year?" asked Benjamin.

"Yep, they do it every year," returned Phyllis. "My parents, the O'Malleys, Uncle Henry and now, Elenore also, are all going. They go to Wisconsin Dells for almost every Labor Day weekend."

"Is that the place where we went that had the boat rides on the river?" inquired Benjamin.

Phyllis told him that it was.

"Must not have been all that much fun for a kid," commented Benjamin. "Especially for a kid that was used to going to crime scenes."

Phyllis giggled, "Actually it was. Back then it wasn't as crowded as when I took you. It was a small town. The adults would go off and do their thing, mostly drinking, and they would leave me to wander around all by myself. It was great. Wisconsin is hunting heaven, they love their guns up there. Just off the main street there was a great little gun shop. It even had a shooting range. They had a bunch of old time cowboy revolvers. They even had a couple of 1917 Colt 45 caliber revolvers with the five and a half inch long barrel. They used to call them 'hog legs' in the old west."

Benjamin laughed, "I'm a history professor, I know what a hog leg is."

Phyllis resumed, "I could spend the entire day there. In the evenings we'd have dinner together and then go to a place called Captain Cook's Showboat Lounge. It was decorated to look like an old time riverboat. They would show old time silent movies and then have a sing-a-long between films. They had a piano player, and two banjo players. It was great! I would flirt with strange boys, and I had my first beer there, I was only twelve."

"I never knew that you were so wild," teased Benjamin.

Phyllis giggled, "It was fun."

"So why didn't you take me to this Captain Cook's when we went there?" wondered Benjamin.

Phyllis blushed and giggled, "If you remember, we had better things to do at night."

Benjamin chuckled, "Did Phillip ever go along?"

Phyllis nodded, "Yep, he and my grandmother always went.  He stopped two years after she died.  I always figured that it just reminded him too much of her."

Benjamin nodded, "I can understand that. Maybe we should have gone with your parents this year."

Phyllis laughed, "You would have to have made that decision back in June in order to get a reservation."

"Why didn't we?" Benjamin asked.

Phyllis shrugged, "It's gotten way too crowded and commercial now.  When I was a kid, it was so small that the four police officers drove Volkswagen Beatles as squad cars."

Benjamin laughed.

"How hick can you get?  Right?" denounced Phyllis.

"So, what do you want to do this weekend?" sighed Benjamin.

Phyllis shook her head, "I don't know. Everything is so crowded on the Labor Day weekend, and everybody's drunk."

"How about a movie?" Benjamin suggested.

"What's playing?" Phyllis asked enthusiastically.

Benjamin thought for a few seconds, "*Dog Day Afternoon*, with Al Pacino.  It's about a bank robbery."

Phyllis cringed, "Too much like work."

"Then there's *The Land that Time Forgot*," Benjamin considered.

"Sounds like one that I'd like to forget," sighed Phyllis.

"Well, there's always *Jaws*.  It's been out for months and we still haven't seen it," reminded Benjamin.

"I don't mind eating fish," Phyllis giggle.  "But the idea of fish eating people is just not for me. How about we just lay in bed late and then see what comes to mind?"

"We could do the Art Institute," grinned Benjamin.

Phyllis smiled, "Yeah, I haven't been there for a while."

"That's because nothing's been stolen from them for a while," Benjamin chuckled.

"Are you trying to say that I don't appreciate fine art?" scolded Phyllis.

Benjamin shook his head, "No, but you really appreciate it most when there's a reward out for it."

Phyllis laughed.  They had arrived at Gulliver's by that time.  They parked the car and crossed the street.  It wasn't as crowded as they expected it to be and were seated immediately.

"Nick and Jane are working cases this weekend and I know Phillip is flying to Atlantic City to gamble.  And Dave and his hooker fiancée are heading to Vegas.  What are Jackie and Duck doing?" Benjamin continued the conversation.

"My God, you must really be desperate for something to do if you're asking about Jackie and Duck," laughed Phyllis.

"No!" protested Benjamin, "I was just curious."

Phyllis smiled, "Gramps has given them the whole week off.  They're sailing to Mackinac Island with Nora and Patterson.  I guess that you're just stuck spending time with the old ball and chain, and not only for the weekend, but also for the entire week!"

Benjamin looked upset, "I love spending time with you.  As a matter of fact, I've been considering quitting my teaching position at the college so that I can work full time at the agency.  That way I can spend more time with you."

Phyllis laughed, "Oh yeah, that'll be the day."

"I'm serious," protested Benjamin.

Phyllis looked confused, "But teaching is all that you've ever wanted to do."

"It's dull and boring," lamented Benjamin.

"Yeah, but that never bothered you in the past," snickered Phyllis.

"I like working at the agency," Benjamin confessed.  "And I love working with you.  I love being a part of your world."

Now Phyllis looked upset, "Ben, you are not just a part of my world!  You are my entire world!"

"And you are my whole world also, and that's why I want to be with you all the time," Benjamin insisted.

Phyllis smiled, "Most married people don't work together."

"Most married people don't have the opportunity to work together.  We do, and so far, it has worked out great," insisted Benjamin.

Phyllis snickered, "Right, I got you shot!"

"I was wearing a vest," reminded Benjamin. "And who was it that saved you from getting killed when Ming Lee's men kidnapped you?"

Phyllis smiled lovingly, "You.  But don't you think that you should be giving this a lot of thought?"

"I have.  Lately my students have been asking me more questions about my cases than about history.  And what's worse is that I like telling them about working as a private investigator.  I even committed the cardinal sin and showed them my gun!" Benjamin said, with embarrassment.

Phyllis laughed aloud, "Gramps would have a hissy fit!"

"My teaching assistant does all the history teaching.  I've even talked to the chancellor of the college," Benjamin admitted.  "And I've talked to your grandfather."

"You seem to have talked to everyone except me about this," Phyllis sighed.

"I've done more than talk," Benjamin squeaked out, "I've done it."

"You quit your job!" exclaimed Phyllis.

"I'll teach this semester, so they have time to replace me.  And I'll still be a guest lecturer from time to time.  The chancellor is aware that I've been having my teaching assistants cover most of my classes.  He said that he was expecting it," Benjamin informed Phyllis.

"Just when were you going to fill me in on all of this?" growled Phyllis.

"That's what I'm doing now," Benjamin moaned. "Or is it that you just don't want me around the office that much? Is it that I'm not that good of a detective?"

Phyllis sighed, "No, you're a great detective. Better than most. In fact, since you're into all that computer stuff, you're what the future of the detective business is becoming."

"Then it's that you like having the time away from me," Benjamin groaned.

"No!" Phyllis snapped. "You should know better than that."

"Then what?" demanded Benjamin softly.

Phyllis looked into Benjamin's eyes, "Ever since I met you, it seems that you have been giving up things for me. You gave up getting a doctorate for me. You gave up living in Los Angeles for me. You gave up working for Uncle Henry at the museum and the university for me. And now you're giving up teaching for me. I've never given up anything for you. And that makes me feel badly."

"You don't have to feel badly about a thing,"
Benjamin insisted.  "You've given me the most
important thing in my life.  You've given me
you.  Don't you realize that if it weren't for
you, I'd be a lonely bachelor spending all his
time in musty old museums, teaching a bunch
of kids who would be laughing at me behind
my back?  All the time I'd be growing old,
alone, reading about other people's lives.
Because of you, I have a life.  I have a rich,
vibrant, exciting life, with a beautiful wife."

Phyllis smiled with tears in her eyes, "Well, in
that case, ok.  You can quit that boring job at
the college and bore us fulltime."

Benjamin smiled, "Phillip said that since I'm
coming on full time, we're going to be getting
computers."

"My God!" gasped Phyllis.  "You're bringing
Phillip Clark into the last half of the twentieth
century?  I don't believe it.  It took me five
years just to get him to buy air conditioners."

"Isn't it great?" Benjamin asked excitedly.

Phyllis started to laugh, "I can't wait to see
Alice using a computer.  I mean, she can't even
make the *Mr. Coffee* work on a timer."

"Well, that's a load off my chest," admitted Benjamin. "But we still don't have any plans for this weekend."

"You know what I'd really like to do?" sighed Phyllis dreamily. "I'd like to spend the three days laying on the sand on the beach on Mormo's Cay in the Bahamas."

"That would be nice," agreed Benjamin. "However, since we sent Doctor Gonzalo's daughter to jail, I really don't think that we'd be very welcomed by him."

"I suppose that we'll just have to sit around like an old married couple," chuckled Phyllis.

Benjamin chuckled slightly, "Tell me more about this Mackinac Island that Duck and Jackie are going to."

Phyllis shrugged, "Mackinac is the French pronunciation. It's called Mackinaw in English. It's an island located in Lake Huron, at the eastern end of the Straits of Mackinac, between the state's Upper and Lower Peninsula. The name of the island in Odawa is Michilimackinac which means 'big turtle'. It was once a British fort but is now mostly a resort area. It is kind of like Santa Catalina off the coast of California, except that it's cold there.  It's less than four and a half square miles and is in the state of Michigan."

"Have you ever been there?" Benjamin asked.

Phyllis nodded, "Mom and Dad took me there once, along with Uncle Henry.  It was pretty cool, and I don't mean temperature wise.  Although, as I remember, the temperature was pretty cool also.  What Uncle Henry liked best was the fact that motorized vehicles have been prohibited on the island since 1898, except for emergency vehicles, city service vehicles, and snowmobiles during winter. The only way to get around is by foot, bicycle, horse, or horse-drawn carriages."

"Sounds like Henry's kind of place," Benjamin laughed.

"Oh, he loved it there," Phyllis chuckled. "What I liked the best when I was a kid is that you could get from the mainland to the island by snowmobiles during winter.  The straight freezes completely over."

"That's kind of scary, if you ask me," moaned Benjamin.  "Maybe we could go there sometime during the summer.  No way am I crossing any part of the Great Lakes over the ice."

Phyllis laughed, "Definitely, the average winter temperature is zero and up to ten below, unlike Catalina."

"Unlike anyplace that any sane person would ever choose to go to," scoffed Benjamin.

"It never gets much over 73 degrees there, and this time of year it gets down to 48. I read that the temperature average expected this weekend is 49 degrees with 82% humidity," Phyllis expressed.

"I was wrong," Benjamin sighed. "Let's not ever go there."

"Especially by snowmobile," agreed Phyllis.

"How far of a sail is it?" Benjamin wondered.

"Three-hundred and thirty-three miles," returned Phyllis quickly.

"And you just happen to know this, why?" asked Benjamin.

"Because there is a yearly race from the Chicago Yacht Club to Mackinac. It usually takes around twenty-eight to thirty hours," Phyllis answered.

"That's a lot longer than I would like to be in the middle of Lake Michigan," whined Benjamin.

"Patterson won't be in the middle of the lake for that long," Phyllis returned. "He'll hug the coast until he gets to Milwaukee and then make the two and a half hour crossing to Muskegon. They'll spend the night there. The next day he'll hug the coast again all the way to Northport and then be on open lake for about a half hour to the island."

Benjamin snickered, "I didn't know that you knew anything about sailing."

"Oh, I don't," Phyllis admitted. "Jackie told me their plans. She said that she'd never have consented to going if they wouldn't be able to see land, except for the Milwaukee to Muskegon part. She is nervous about that part."

"I don't blame her," admitted Benjamin. "I don't really trust that Patterson character."

Phyllis shrugged, "I guess that he's been sailing all his life."

# Chapter Three

# A Sunday Afternoon in the Park

It was heavily overcast when Phyllis and Benjamin awoke Saturday, August 30th.  A quick glance out the bedroom window confirmed that it was, indeed, raining.

"That figures, three days off and it's going to rain the whole time.  It's the last real weekend of summer!" complained Benjamin.

"I wonder if it's raining up at Wisconsin Dells?" sighed Phyllis.

Actually, in Wisconsin Dells it had drizzled lightly between four and six in the morning. The temperature would hover between sixty and sixty-eight with heavy cloud cover all day. But it didn't matter to those who were there, as it just meant spending the whole day shuffling from one tavern to the next, and that is exactly what they would have done if it had been bright and sunny.  The next two days had no rain, however, on September first, the temperature got as high as eighty-three and as low as fifty-two.

"I'm glad that we didn't make any plans that involved being outside for any length of time," grumbled Benjamin looking out the window at the rain coming down.

"I'm sure happy that we didn't go sailing with Patterson and Nora.  There's no place worse than being on a small boat in the rain," moaned Phyllis.

"Yes, there is," refuted Benjamin.

Phyllis looked at him in anticipation.

"A tent!" pronounced Benjamin.

"The only time that I've ever been in a tent is when we were looking for the devil's scepter," commented Phyllis.

"Henry and I were doing research on the old goldrush towns around Columbia State Park in Tuolumne, California.  It's just north of Sonora in the Sierra Nevada foothills.  Actually, you and I passed it on our way to Mount Judah when we were searching for the devil's scepter."  Benjamin went on, "When Henry and I were working there, it rained for days.  It was miserable.  And when it stopped raining, everything was a muddy mess.  I can't imagine a wet boat being worse than that was.  It was the worst expedition that I was ever on."

"What was the best expedition that you were ever on?" asked Phyllis.

"Searching for the Devil's Scepter with you," Benjamin returned quickly.

Phyllis smiled, "Good answer!"

Benjamin chuckled, "You are everyone of my best times ever."

"I feel the same way," Phyllis purred contentedly.  "I know that I'm your very best times ever."

Benjamin chuckled, "May I remind you that you are also responsible for the scariest times that I've ever had."

"We won't talk about those," Phyllis snickered.

Since the rain had slowed down to a very light drizzle, and the sun was attempting to show itself, the two decided to have breakfast at the corner diner.

"How's the new married couple doing," asked their usual waitress.

"I don't know if we qualify as 'the new married couple' anymore, we've been married nearly fifteen months," replied Phyllis.

The waitress laughed.

Phyllis and Benjamin ordered chili-cheese omelets, English muffins, orange juice and coffee.

After their breakfast, the rain had stopped, so they decided to take public transportation to the Art Institute.  Parking was always difficult anywhere in the downtown area.  It was just a short walk from the diner to the elevated train station.  Once downtown, you could go right from the "L" platform into a store, then cut through that store to the Michigan Avenue side, and just cross the street to the museum.  So, they felt safe from any unexpected down pours. They arrived at the Art Institute chilly, but dry.

"There is this great painting," announced Phyllis enthusiastically.  "I don't remember if I showed it to you any of the other times that we've been here.  It's so cool!  It's made up of thousands of little dots of paint."

"*Sunday Afternoon on the Island of Grand Jatte*, by Georges Seurat," chuckled Benjamin. "I have seen it, the first time that I came to Chicago with Henry.  You showed it to me then.  And you're right, it is very cool."

The two headed toward the galleries where the neo-impressionists were displayed but were sadly disappointed to find no "cool" *Sunday Afternoon on the Island of Grand Jatte.*

Phyllis asked one of the guards what had happened to it.  He was an older man, and even looked familiar to Phyllis.

"Miss Clark," the guard recognized her.  "It's good to see you."

Phyllis was surprised that he knew her.  But he had remembered her from when she and Phillip had recovered the *Stars of Bethlehem*, in 1967.

"Good memory!" exclaimed Phyllis.  "That was eight years ago.  It's Mrs. Attlee now."

Phyllis introduced Benjamin and they quickly chatted about the *Stars of Bethlehem* robbery for a few minutes.  Then the guard explained that the *Sunday Afternoon on the Island of Grand Jatte* had taken a vacation.

"It's the second time since 1924 that it's been out of our museum," he explained.  "I would suppose that it's on a train somewhere between here and New York right now."

Phyllis expressed her disappointment and the two ventured on to another gallery.

The guard was right, the painting was, at that moment, in one of a hundred fifteen cars making up a train that was sitting on a siding east of Harrisburg Pennsylvania, waiting for a west bound freight train to pass.

The rest of the day the temperature stayed between sixty-eight and seventy degrees.  It was raining when Phyllis and Benjamin left the Art Institute at six, when it closed.  They quickly made their way across Michigan Avenue and into the shelter of one of the stores on the west side of the street.

"It would figure, it only rains in Chicago on holiday weekends," complained Phyllis.

A half inch of rain fell between five and nine that evening.  Not a record by any means but annoying, none the less.  The wet couple got on board a north bound Ravenswood elevated train and headed for their warm, dry apartment.

It was late morning, Sunday, August 31st, when Patterson docked his sailboat in the yacht basin at Mackinac Island.  It was fifty-eight degrees as Jackie huddled under a blanket next to the helm as Patterson navigated.  Nora and Duck were asleep below deck.

"We're here," advised Patterson.

Jackie looked around, "Looks quaint."

Patterson nodded, "Maybe we should get a couple of hours sleep before we wake the others."

Jackie nodded, "You should sleep. I'm afraid that I wasn't very good company for you. I know that I drifted off a few times during the night."

Patterson smiled, "That's ok. Before you go below, I wanted to thank you once again for what you did for my aunt, and especially for saving my life. I can't believe that you actually killed someone for me."

Jackie smiled at Patterson, "It's just part of the job."

Patterson looked sincerely grateful, "I don't believe that anyone would have done what you did for me. Most people really don't like me very much, certainly not enough to save my life."

"If it had been Duck that was following you that day, he would have done the same thing," Jackie replied.

Patterson shook his head, "If it weren't for you, Duck would never have gotten involved with me. I was always such an ass to everyone, especially Duck."

"Duck's not the same person that he was in high school.  Actually, neither am I.  The Clarks have made such a difference in our lives."

"I really love Nora," Patterson sighed.  "I would like to have the kind of relationship that you and Duck have."

"It looks like you're doing alright from what I can see," Jackie reassured.

"I'm never sure if a girl likes me or my money," moaned Patterson.

Jackie laughed, "Oh, Pat.  No one has enough money to make a girl put up with a personality like yours, unless she really loves the guy."

Patterson chuckled, "I suppose that you're right.  You know, even with all my money, I still admire you and Duck."

Jackie looked at Patterson inquisitively.

"The two of you make a difference," Patterson said.  "You make peoples' lives better.  You help people.  I would like to be a part of something like that."

Jackie looked surprised, "Are you saying that that you would rather be a private investigator than a journalist?"

Patterson shrugged, "I don't really know what I want to do.  I'm just saying that I envy the two of you.  I really doubt that I could ever shoot anybody.  I just don't have the nerve."

"I never thought that I could shoot anyone, but when push comes to shove, and you know what's on the line, you do what you have to do.  It's after it's all over that you get sick to your stomach," Jackie explained.

Patterson sighed hard, "I'm such a wimp."

Jackie sat quietly for a few moments, "I heard Professor Attlee and Mr. Clark talking about putting in a computer system.  That sounds like it would be right up your alley.  Maybe you should talk to Professor Attlee."

Patterson smiled and nodded.

In Chicago, Sunday proved to be a much dryer day.  Phyllis and Benjamin decided to spend the slightly overcast Sunday afternoon in the park.  They drove to Lincoln Park and parked near the zoo, just south of Fullerton Avenue.  This was not far from where Duck and Jackie had chased down the psychopath, Angie Gatling, just about a month earlier.

"One thing that I don't like about our business is that there doesn't seem to be any place in this city that we can go that doesn't bring to mind some sort of gunfight," grumbled Benjamin.

"At least we weren't involved in this one," consoled Phyllis.

"Yeah, but wasn't that the bench where the police found Matias Santino Herrera?" groaned Benjamin pointing to a park bench.

Phyllis nodded, "One of those Argentinians that was after Helena's Cross?  I think that it was."

"He was the Brazilian," corrected Benjamin.

Phyllis nodded, "That's right.  Considering the fact that everywhere that we go reminds you of a case, are you sure that you really want to do this full time?"

Benjamin chuckled and hugged his wife, "All good memories, My Dear."

"Me, getting kidnapped twice, you, getting shot once, and, Gramps, nearly getting killed can't be good memories!" Phyllis reminded.

"Yeah, but it all turned out alright," Benjamin sighed.

The two walked under the bridle path bridge with the statue of General Grant above it and entered the southern most part of the zoo.  On this side of the hill was a small lagoon where people went rowing.

"I can't take you sailing like Patterson takes Nora, but how about rowing?" asked Benjamin.

Phyllis smiled, "As long as you do all the rowing!"

Benjamin said that he would and the two went down to the boathouse to rent a rowboat.

"You know, if you wanted to get a boat, we can certainly afford it," Phyllis told Benjamin as he started to row away from the small pier.

Benjamin looked at her with surprise, "What makes you think that I'd want a boat?"

"You were raised in Southern California, not far from the ocean," Phyllis considered. "Isn't everyone out there into surfing, swimming, and boating?"

Benjamin chuckled and shook his head, "Not everyone. If you remember, I wasn't exactly the suntanned surfer boy when we met."

"We went to the beach," Phyllis reminded him.

"And laid on the sand drinking *mie ties* with Henry," Benjamin concurred. "In fact, yes, I hated going in the ocean. There's things in there that can eat you.  Not to mention all the bacteria and sewage.”

“Now you tell me!” exclaimed Phyllis.

“I never learned to surf or sail,” Benjamin continued.  “I did like to swim, but only in nice clean, heavily chlorinated pools.”

Phyllis laughed.

“I guess that I’m just not the outdoorsy kind of guy,” admitted Benjamin.  “I would have never gone camping if Henry hadn’t insisted that I go on his expeditions with him.  I never went hunting or fishing.”

“Oh, I beg to correct you, Love,” Phyllis snickered.  “You have gone hunting, only not for animals.  We do it all the time.”

“That’s a totally different thing,” Benjamin confessed.  “And yes, I do love the chase.”

Phyllis pointed to a far corner of the lagoon where there were extremely high reeds and dense foliage.

“Go that way,” Phyllis instructed.

“Why?” asked Benjamin.

Phyllis blushed and giggled, “There’s a little cove back there that’s screened from sight.

Most people don't know that it's there.  It's a
great place to make out."

Benjamin smiled, "And how do you come to
know about this hide-away?  I thought that you
never had a boyfriend before me."

Phyllis giggled, "I didn't.  I only know about it
because Uncle Sean once found a body there."

Benjamin shook his head and laughed, "We're
going to go make out where Sean found a dead
body.  How romantic!"

"It's really out of the way and secluded,"
protested Phyllis.

"Hence the reason that the body was left there,"
insisted Benjamin.  "With our luck we'll
probably find another one there today."

"If we do, we'll just row away, forget about it,
and find somewhere else to kiss," Phyllis
snickered.

Benjamin shook his head, "No we won't.  One
of us will go call Jack Flynn while the other
preserves the integrity of the crime scene.  Then
we'll spend the rest of the weekend in some
sort of murder investigation."

Phyllis laughed, "I promise!  If there's a body
in there, I'll pretend that I never saw it.  In fact,

I'll keep my eyes closed until you're satisfied that there are no dead people anywhere to be seen."

Benjamin laughed and rowed for the secluded cove.  There were no dead or other living bodies.

# Chapter Four

# A Sunday Afternoon in New York?

It was one-thirty-seven in the morning on Monday, when the special boxcar arrived behind a little GE 44 ton, center cab switching engine at the underground receiving dock of the Museum of Modern Art. It was fifty-five hours after the time that it had left its home at the Chicago Art Institute. The guards had made the last few miles of the trip inside the boxcar with the painting.

The little engine carried its precious cargo over track 61 and track 63. These tracks, completely underground, ran from the Grand Central Terminal and were originally built to carry freight and serve as loading platforms for a steam powerhouse that once existed on 49th Street. They were eventually switched over for passenger use. But they were not ever used for ordinary passenger service. Beginning in 1929, these tracks carried the rich and famous in their private rail cars to places like the Waldorf-Astoria Hotel. In 1938 the *New York Times* did an article about General John J. Pershing arriving by this route. Although there is only one documented instance that mentions that President Roosevelt made use of Track 61, it is generally believed that it was used many times, but kept secret for national security reasons. On October 21, 1944, Roosevelt made a campaign stop in New York City.  A Secret Service memorandum states "At 10:05 p.m., the President will leave the hotel over the same route he entered, i.e., via east side Lexington Avenue elevator, and will then proceed via New York Central elevators to the New York Central Rail siding, located in the basement of the hotel.".

People who've worked at the Waldorf-Astoria Hotel whisper of dozens of famous people that had arrived the very same way, and anyone who had worked in the museums and galleries of Manhattan knew about the secret arrivals of precious items by way of the underground tunnels.  Seurat's painting was in good company as it made its way from the Penn Central's freight yard, along the legendary tracks 61 and 63, to the Museum of Modern Art.  Upon its arrival the Chicago Art Institute's guards were joined by guards from the Museum of Modern Art and a squad of New York City police.  Museum workers unloaded the painting from its special boxcar and transported it up to the very secure receiving area of the basement of the museum where it would wait until

Tuesday morning, when the director of the museum would supervise its uncrating and unwrapping before taking it up to the second floor for display.  The Chief of Security for the Museum of Modern Art signed the paper accepting responsibility for the painting and the Chicago guards rode the boxcar back to the Grand Central Station.  They then caught an Amtrak train back to Chicago.  Their job was done. The painting had arrived safely at its destination in New York without any incident.

Just about the time that the famous painting was arriving at the Museum of Modern Art, Benjamin was rolling over in bed.

Monday morning the Attlees slept late again. They once again grabbed breakfast at the diner near where they lived and then drove to Lincoln Park.  This time they brought a picnic basket with submarine sandwiches.  They parked on Simonds Drive across from the boat docking at Montrose Harbor and walked up the hill to a stand of trees.  From this spot they could see the boats moored in the little harbor to the north and the Chicago skyline to the south.  It was less than a hundred yards from where the third victim of the Monday Morning Murderer had been found.  Both Phyllis and Benjamin knew that this was the spot.  But neither of them mentioned it.  But, of course, Benjamin, having been a history professor, did mention the fact that the reason that the hill that they were now sitting on even existed was because it covered a missel silo that had existed from 1962 through 1967.

"It had been put in around the time of the Cuban Missile crisis to shoot down any missiles aimed at Chicago," Benjamin told Phyllis.

Phyllis smiled and chuckled a little, "Are you really sure that you want to give up teaching history?"

Benjamin chuckled also, "Just because I'm not going to be teaching any more doesn't mean that I have to forget everything that I know."

"Maybe you can forget just a little bit of what you know?" laughed Phyllis.

"It's hard to forget that time period," Benjamin returned.

Phyllis nodded, "Yeah, I know.  I remember being in school.  I was eleven years old.  We had nuclear attack drills.  They did these simulations.  We'd be sitting in class and all of a sudden the air raid sirens would go off and we would have to stop everything and crawl under our desks and listen to jets flying overhead at low altitude.  It was really frightening.  There was this one time that they hustled us all down to the school's sub-basement where we sat on the cold floor for about an hour.  At least we couldn't hear the jets flying over.  It was cold and dark and damp down there.  All the kids were terrified.  I remember one of the kids whispering that his father had been in the Navy during World War Two and told him that he had seen the after effects of the Atomic bomb attack on Hiroshima.  His father had told him that it was better not to survive.  That really made all of us feel really good.  I told Gramps how scared I was.  He said that he would protect me.  Funny, I believed him and never felt scared again.  I guess that I was just a stupid little kid.  Somehow I figured that Gramps would shoot down the missiles with his 'Tommy Gun'."

Benjamin looked at Phyllis, "In L. A. we just ignored it all and went about our business.  I guess that everyone remembered the panic in California when Pearl Harbor got attacked and figured that they just weren't going to go crazy again."

# Chapter Five

## Back to Work

It was nine Tuesday morning when both Phyllis and Benjamin arrived at the office.  Since Saint Olis Ritt University didn't resume classes until mid-September, Benjamin would work full time with Phyllis.  Alice was at the reception desk. Phillip had arrived at eight-thirty and was pouring a cup of coffee when the two arrived.

"Well, how was your weekend?" Phillip asked politely.

Benjamin and Phyllis smiled and told him that it had been nice.

"Did you see in the papers that there was a bus robbery Sunday?" Phillip asked.

Both Benjamin and Phyllis shook their heads as they also poured cups of coffee.

"It was a modern version of an old stagecoach holdup.  Two armed bandits were among the thirty-eight passengers on a Greyhound bus from Chicago enroute to Toronto.  Just before they got to Detroit they pulled their roscoes and commenced to relieve the passengers of twenty grand in cash and around fifteen grand in valuables.  They then got off the bus in a secluded area and disappeared.  Not a bad day's work."

"Not bad at all," mused Phyllis.

"Gotta give them credit for going old school. Ain't been nothing like that in a long time," Phillip snickered.

"Did you see that a Concorde flew across the Atlantic four times in one day, yesterday?" Benjamin asked.

"No, I didn't catch that.  That's gotta be some kind of record," exclaimed Phillip.

"Yeah, it's the first time ever," confirmed Benjamin.  "It took off from London and flew to Gander, Newfoundland in two hours and nineteen minutes.  They then refueled it and it went right back.  Did it twice in thirteen hours and fifty-nine minutes.  Nine thousand, five hundred miles total."

Phillip looked astonished, "Fourteen hours!  I remember when it used to take that many days to get from New York to England."

"That's the southern route, the Queen Mary used to make it direct in a week," Benjamin corrected.

"How fast does that danged plane go?" Phillip exclaimed.

"Two hours and nineteen minutes," repeated Benjamin. "That's around twelve hundred miles an hour."

Phillip shook his head, "Way too fast if you ask me.  Spending time alone on a ship with someone you love was the reason for going in my day."

"Still is, Gramps," agreed Phyllis.  "I can't imagine having the luxury of spending fourteen days all alone, uninterrupted, with Ben, without anyone calling to say that something's been stolen, or someone's run off or been killed."

Benjamin laughed, "Really?  We couldn't figure out what to do over a long weekend!"

Phillip laughed, "Your grandmother and I never had any problems knowing what to do."

Phyllis blushed and giggled.

"Oh," snickered Phillip.  "And the really big news is that Dave called me early this morning. He ain't coming in for the rest of the week."

"Don't tell me," chuckled Phyllis.

"I knew it," laughed Benjamin.

"Yep," Phillip snickered. "He did it. He and Kat tied the knot."

Seven hundred and thirteen miles east, the director of the Museum of Modern Art eagerly stood in the basement work area of the museum watching as his workmen carefully removed the wooden boards that made up the packing crate of the *Sunday Afternoon on the Island of Grand Jatte*. Once the sides, top and front were removed, the painting was supported by the back of the crate, leaning against a wall of the workroom. Now the workers began removing the special, fireproof, soft protective wrapping, even more carefully. The wrapping was made of a material that could not harm the surface of the painting in any way. It was nonabrasive and acid free. The director actually held his breath as the protective covering fell to the floor to reveal a seven foot by ten foot framed white canvas with the words "Forty million dollars will get your painting back", painted on it in black paint. The director nearly passed out.

Back in Chicago, Benjamin sat in Phillip's office discussing the prospect of connecting to the budding Ethernet, especially to the newly developing Chicago Police Department data base.

"It all started in 1960 when the University of Illinois created PLATO, the Programed Logic for Automatic Teaching Operations.  This allowed students throughout the school and all of its campuses to access the universities mainframe computer to do research and to get help in their classes," Benjamin told Phillip.  "But the idea of a real network didn't become real until October 29th,1969, when UCLA's Network Measurement Center, Stanford Research Institute, University of California-Santa Barbara, and University of Utah all installed, what they called nodes.  The first message ever sent was simply "LO" sent by a student named Charles Kline."

"LO?" interrupted Phillip.

"Actually he was attempting to send 'login' to the Stanford Research Institute's computer, but he couldn't finish because the Stanford Research Institute's computer system crashed," Benjamin explained.

"This sounds really promising," groaned Phillip.

Benjamin chuckled, "It gets substantially better. In 1973 global networking became a reality when the University College of London and the Royal Radar Establishment in Norway connected to a network called ARPANET. At the same time a company named Vadic, introduced the *VA3400* modem, which was able to transmit 1,200 bits over a normal phone line. Because of this invention the Xerox company was able to set up the Ethernet. Using all this new technology, a commercial version of ARPANET, known as Telenet, became the first Internet Service Provider for use by people like us just last year."

Phillip listened attentively to Benjamin.

"That's all very interesting, at least what I can understand of it. But how is any of this useful to us?" Phillip wondered.

"While all this was happening in the world of computer technology, existing computers were coming into use everywhere for bookkeeping and file storage, including police departments," replied Benjamin.

Phillip's face brightened considerably, "Now we're getting somewhere."

"Right!" Benjamin agreed. "On November 29th, 1971, the Computerized Criminal History Program began to operate. This is a system where wanted persons and stolen property files are maintained in the National Crime

Information Center, The NCIC had begun collecting and storing files in 1967, but because of the technology available at the time, it did very little good.  However, now with the Ethernet, those files are accessible to anyone who has a modem and a computer terminal.  In addition, anyone with a computer terminal can access files and information kept at most major colleges, Universities, and even many libraries. Of course, you need to know how to do it."

"And, I take it that you know how to do it," stated Phillip.

Benjamin smiled, "That's what I've been doing whenever you send me out to do research."

Phillip chuckled, "And I always thought that you were just really smart."

Benjamin laughed, "It does take a degree of skill."

"Ok, I'm sold," Phillip said excitedly.  "How do we get one of them modem thingies and a terminal, so we can get ourselves hooked up to the Ethernet thingamabob?  And what will it cost?"

"Xerox makes a computer terminal called the Alto, after their development lab in Palo Alto, California.  It's a groundbreaking little computer.  We can down load files from the NCIC and the Chicago Police Department along with other places.  We can keep our own files and send them to the police and to anyone who has a computer terminal!  We can do payroll and even print checks with it," Benjamin went on excitedly.  "The downside is that to get everything that we need, it will cost somewhere in the neighborhood of twelve to thirty-two thousand dollars."

Phillip leaned back into his swivel chair, "That's some neighborhood.  There goes Phyllis' inheritance."

"We'll be more productive than ever," Benjamin reminded.  "Some of the menial things that take Nick, Dave, and Jane days to run down can be done on the computer by Alice."

Phillip snickered, "Alice can't even make coffee.  Let's hope that Nora can learn this stuff."

Just then Alice buzzed Phillip on the intercom.

"Speak of the devil," Phillip sighed.  "Took her a month to learn how do use the intercom.  She still can't transfer a call."

Alice informed Phillip that the Thomas Jefferson Insurance Company was on line one. Phillip took the call.  There was no expression on his face as he listened and spoke.  Benjamin listened to half of a conversation.  He could tell by what he was hearing that something expensive had disappeared.

"Yes, in fact it was my granddaughter who recovered the *Stars of Bethlehem*, the *Emerald Isle*, and the *Dachimer Blue*."  Phillip told the caller.

At this, Benjamin surmised that they were about to be getting a jewelry case from the insurance company.  He was wrong.  Phillip finally agreed to take the case and hung-up the phone.  Benjamin stared at Phillip in anticipation.

Phillip looked back, "Get your wife."

Benjamin quickly opened the door to Phyllis' office and called her.

"I don't know anything about computers and whatever you guys decide is fine with me," Phyllis called back and then mumbled to herself something about her not being able to get him to buy air conditioners.

"Your grandfather wants you about a case," Benjamin called again.

This time Phyllis got up and went into Phillip's office.

"That was the Thomas Jefferson Insurance Company," Phillip began. "It seems that some world famous painting has gone missing, somewhere between here and the Big Apple, and you've been chosen to find it."

Phyllis smiled. "I've never worked the theft of a painting before."

"But you have recovered some of the most high profile rocks ever lifted," returned Phillip.

"So, what went missing?" Phyllis asked, still smiling contentedly with her reputation.

"Some doohickey by some Frog. 'Sunday in the Park' or something like that," Phillip answered.

"*Sunday Afternoon on the Island of Grand Jatte*?" exclaimed Phyllis.

Phillip nodded, "Yeah, that's it."

"My God, that is big!" exclaimed Benjamin.

"You guys have heard of it?" Phillip wondered. "Of course, Benjamin has, but you too?"

Phyllis nodded, "It's one of the most famous
works of art in the world.  Everyone's heard of
it."

"Or at least have seen a copy of it," added
Benjamin.  "But most people mistakenly call it
Sunday Afternoon in the Park."

"What is a 'Jatte' anyway?" Phillip wondered.

Phyllis looked at Benjamin.

"Literally, jatte is French for bowl," Benjamin
offered.

"So, the painting is Sunday afternoon on the
Island of big bowl?" asked Phyllis.

"Literally," smirked Benjamin.  "However, the
painting is of a pastoral island park on the river
Seine, just outside the gates of Paris.  For many
years after his painting was done, it had turned
into an industrial site.  But mostly because of
Seurat's painting becoming so famous, it has
been refurbished into a public garden and a
high end housing development."

"We were just at the Art Institute Saturday.  We
were going to see it, but one of the guards
informed us that it was going to New York for
display," Phyllis inserted.

"Well, it didn't make it there!" advised Phillip.

"The thing is huge!" exclaimed Benjamin. "It's actually bigger than my office here."

"Alright, alright," Phillip snickered. "I know that you've got a tiny office. But you gotta remember you were only working part time, and Jackie and Duck don't even have offices. I couldn't toss Nick, Dave, or Jane out of their offices. They've been with me for years. I'm looking into renting the accountant's office next-door so we can expand. OK?"

Benjamin chuckled slightly, "I wasn't complaining. I was just saying that it is actually bigger than my office. It's seven foot by ten foot."

Phillip was shocked, "How in the devil do you steal a painting that's that big?"

"Usually an art thief cuts the painting out of its frame and just rolls it up and walks off with it," replied Phyllis.

"But even at that, it's either seven feet long or ten feet long, depending on how you roll it," rebuffed Phillip. "Someone had to see something that big being carried off."

Phyllis and Benjamin shrugged.

"Well, they want you in New York," Phillip informed them. "The two of you catch a flight out as soon as you can. There's a lot of money in this for us. This piece is valued at over one hundred twenty million dollars. That's a pretty nice piece of change if you recover it. We could buy a dozen of them Alto doohickies."

Benjamin smiled as Phyllis turned to him in confusion.

"Alto doohickies?" Phyllis wondered.

"I'll tell you on the plane," Benjamin returned as they left the office.

# Chapter Six

# The Big Apple

It was early afternoon when the Attlees checked into their suite at the Martinique Hotel on 32nd Street and Broadway on the lower end of Manhattan.  Alice had specifically chosen this hotel because she thought that Benjamin would like it.

"This is incredible!" exclaimed Benjamin as they went up to their suite.

Phyllis smiled with delight, "Alice knew that you would love this place.  It's one of the oldest hotels in New York.  In fact, it's one of the oldest hotels east of the Mississippi."

Benjamin gazed around in awe, "You don't see places like this anymore."

"And it's just a short cab ride up Sixth Avenue from 32nd Street to 53rd Street where the Museum of Modern Art is located," added Phyllis.

"From the looks of the traffic out there, I doubt that there is any such thing as a 'short' cab ride in this city.  I thought that Chicago was bad, but this…." groaned Benjamin.

Phyllis laughed, "You know, we're only about a block from the Empire State Building."

"And the Museum of Modern Art is just six and a half blocks from Central Park.  I checked it out," added Benjamin.  "The Tavern on the Green is in Central Park at 66th Street and Central Park West."

"Now you sound like Gramps, he'd know where every tavern was," chuckled Phyllis.

"It's not just a tavern, it's part of history," returned Benjamin.  "It was designed by Calvert Vaux in 1880 to house 700 sheep that grazed in Central Park.  In 1934 the sheep were moved to Prospect Park in Brooklyn and the barn was converted to a restaurant by Robert Moses.  It's one of the most famous restaurants in the world."

Phyllis laughed, "All this coming from the guy that has just given up teaching history.  Come on, we've got work to do, Dear."

The two caught a cab on Sixth Street. Benjamin was right, there is no such thing as a quick cab ride in Manhattan.  By the time that they arrived at the Museum of Modern Art it was late afternoon.  They were eagerly greeted by the museum director, and not so eagerly greeted by Lieutenant Mario Santini of the New York Police Department.  The two were quickly escorted down to where the crate was still sitting.

"We got statements from all the workers and guards that were present at the scene," advised Lieutenant Santini.

Phyllis nodded, "I suspect that everything was absolutely normal until they got to the unwrapping of the protective padding."

The lieutenant nodded, "We tried to dust for prints, but the crate's wood is rough and makes it impossible to lift anything,"

"It wouldn't have mattered if it were smooth as glass.  Anyone who could pull off something like this would never leave prints, or anything else."

The Lieutenant agreed.

"I would imagine that it was never out of the sight of these very trustworthy guards at any time since it was unloaded," Phyllis stated.

The Lieutenant nodded.

"Can we see the tunnel where it arrived from?" Phyllis asked.

The Lieutenant chuckled, "Sure can.  But the guards from Chicago were with it every second since it left the Art Institute in Chicago.  If you ask me, it was either snatched back in Chicago or on the way here."

The Lieutenant escorted the Attlees down to the train dock level.  A guard opened the heavy roll up door.  Phyllis and Benjamin peered out into the darkness of the New York underground.

"How extensive is this tunnel network?" Benjamin wondered.

The Lieutenant snickered, "If you laid them all out in a straight line they would run all the way to Saint Louis.  In addition to the railroad lines, there are 36 subway lines, and 472 stations down here.  You're gonna need a lot of people if you want to search it all."

"You mean that you haven't done that already?" Phyllis teased.

Lieutenant Santini returned, "If it were up to the museum director, we'd be doing that right now!"

Phyllis and Benjamin laughed.

Lieutenant Santini smirked, "Just between you and me, I got murders and real crime up the ying-yang.  I don't need, or care, about missing works of art.  The only reason that I have any interest in this at all is that it's bad 'P R' for my city, and we got enough of that as it is."

Phyllis sighed, "I don't blame you.  But I think that you're off the hook for this one.  You're right.  It happened long before it got here.  Where is the boxcar that it was hauled here in?"

"Over in the rail yard in Hoboken," replied the Lieutenant.  "That's in New Jersey."

Phyllis and Benjamin thanked the Lieutenant for his time and patience and went to the Tavern on the Green for dinner.

"I don't expect to see anything of value in Hoboken, but we have got to cover everything," explained Phyllis.  "Plus, checking out Hoboken gives us a reason to spend another day in New York."

"There's no way that the painting could have been taken without the guards seeing what happened," added Benjamin.  "How do you get a two hundred pound, seven foot by eight foot painting, still in its frame, off of a moving train?"

"The train wasn't moving the entire time," corrected Phyllis.

"That being so, the guards should have been extra vigilant whenever it stopped," returned Benjamin.

"Unless it was the guards that took it," suggested Phyllis.

Benjamin looked at his wife questioningly.

"It bothers me that the painting wasn't just cut out of the frame," sighed Phyllis.  "That's what most art thieves do.  But it devalues the painting.  This was taken by people that respect art.  And then there's the fact that they aren't even trying to fence it.  They are holding it for ransom."

"Can you imagine the headache that an exchange like that is going to be?" moaned Benjamin.

Phyllis smiled, "Oh, it might not be as bad as all that."

Benjamin shook his head.

The two ate at the *Tavern on the Green* and returned to their historic hotel.

The next morning Benjamin and Phyllis took a cab to the Penn Central railyards in Hoboken, New Jersey.  It took a few minutes for the yard master to locate the specially equipped boxcar from Chicago, but he eventually did.

"It's being stored on a siding until the cargo is ready for the return trip," explained the yard master. "There's not much call for cars like that one."

The yardmaster led the detectives to where the Art Institute's special car was awaiting its return home. Benjamin and Phyllis opened the car and searched its emptiness. There were no signs of tampering.

"If you ask me," offered the yardmaster, "for my money, the painting was stolen using a helicopter."

Phyllis and Benjamin looked at the yardmaster in disbelief.

The man nodded, "Easy-peasy, if you ask me. The chopper lowers a couple of guys down to the roof. They cut a hole in the roof and attach a cable to the painting. Then the chopper just lifts the painting out of the car."

"What about the hole?" asked Benjamin.

The yardmaster thought for a second, "The guys that did it just stay on board and patch up the hole. They wait until the train comes to a siding and just jump off while it's waiting for another train to pass it."

Phyllis and Benjamin exhaled hard.

"I suppose that we should check the roof, to be on the safe side," groaned Phyllis.

The two climbed up onto the roof of the boxcar. There was no signs of tampering.  Upon coming down they thanked the yardmaster for his help and left for their hotel.  They spent one more night in Manhattan, taking in Rockefeller Center.  It was impossible to get tickets to any Broadway shows.

As the two enjoyed the cafe at Rockefeller Center, Benjamin commented that they should visit Manhattan around Christmas sometime.

"Did you know that they have ice-skating here from Thanksgiving until mid-January every year?" asked Phyllis.

Benjamin chuckled, "Yes, I did know that."

"Of course, you know everything," grumbled Phyllis as she sipped her coffee.

That night they made a conference call to Phillip to see if he had interviewed the Art Institute guards.  He had.

"I interviewed the guards as soon as they got off the train from New York," Phillip apprised them. "They all say that at least one of them had eyes on the car every moment of the trip. They went on to tell me that whenever the train stopped, they all got off and watched the car from every angle. It stopped in Harrisburg, Pennsylvania for a substantial length of time. It was stopped there for an hour and a half, so they got out and opened the boxcar to check on the painting. They say that it was alright."

"Are they absolutely sure that it was the same crate that actually left the Art Institute?" asked Benjamin.

"The man in charge has been around the block a time or two. He doesn't trust anyone. He told me that he put his mark on the crate in an inconspicuous place. That's what he checked for every time he got the chance. He also says that the mark was still there when they unloaded the crate in New York," Phillip assured.

"Then either they are lying, or the painting never left Chicago," Phyllis sighed.

"We know the guy," Phillip added. "He was working there back when the *Stars of Bethlehem* were lifted. He's almost ready for retirement.  Why would he risk his pension and the rest of his life on such a risky proposition?”

“Forty-million dollars is a pretty good reason, if you ask me,” grumbled Benjamin.

“Have there been any more details on the ransom?” wondered Phyllis.

“No!  And that’s got me puzzled.  If it were me, I’d want to get my hands on the cash as soon as I could.  It’s got to be a bear to hide something that big,” Phillip returned.

“Maybe that’s why they haven’t made any more demands yet,” expressed Benjamin.  “They need time to set up the exchange.”

“Could be,” sighed Phillip.  “If they know our history with the Art Institute, they won’t want Phyllis anywhere near the exchange.”

“Then they should do it while I’m in New York,” commented Phyllis.

“Maybe the ransom is only a red herring.  It could be that they’re biding their time, looking for a buyer,” considered Phillip.

“In any case we need to go over the Art Institute with a fine tooth comb,” insisted Phyllis.  “You’re probably right that the guards are telling the truth.  But something just isn't right about all this."

"Just to be thorough, the two of you better fly down to Harrisburg, Pennsylvania and check out that siding where the train stopped for that ninety minutes.  That's enough time for anything to disappear if you ask me," instructed Phillip.

Phyllis and Benjamin agreed.

# Chapter Seven

## One More Day Away

Thursday morning, September 4th, Benjamin and Phyllis checked out of the Martinique Hotel.  They arranged for the hotel limousine to take them the seven and a half miles to LaGuardia Airport.  From LaGuardia they flew the 162 miles to the Harrisburg Airport, which was actually in Middleton, Pennsylvania, nine miles southeast of Harrisburg.  The flight took forty-nine minutes.  After renting a car and getting a map, they drove northwest to the railroad yard near the Susquehanna River.  Once they arrived at the railroad yard the yard superintendent introduced them to his assistant.  The assistant yard superintendent was happy to take them by jeep out to the siding where the eastbound Penn Central train had been held waiting for the westbound freight to pass it early Sunday morning.

"The siding that we're going to is on the river side of US route 22, right next to the Susquehanna River.  It's right alongside The Boyd Big Tree Preserve Conservation Area.  The terrain gets pretty rough in that area and it's usually damp and muddy," the assistant explained.

It took the better part of an hour for them to reach the siding.  It was damp and muddy with tall grass and large rocks.  It would have been impossible to reach with an ordinary vehicle.  The assistant finally pulled up to the spot where the track switched from the main line onto the siding.

"This is where the train turned off to wait," announced the assistant.  "This siding can accommodate one hundred and fifty standard size rail cars."

"So where would you estimate the museum car would have been when the train stopped?" wondered Phyllis.

The assistant looked thoughtful and mumbled some figures inaudibly for a few moments and then began driving slowly while watching his odometer.  After a short distance he stopped.

"It should have been just about here, give or take a few yards," he offered.

Phyllis and Benjamin got out of the jeep and began to walk toward the track.

"Be careful," warned their guide.  "There could be water moccasins around here.  They're poisonous."

Phyllis and Benjamin proceeded very cautiously.  It wasn't hard to discern that there were no tire tracks pressed into the muddy ground.  Nor were there any signs that any vehicle, especially a truck, had depressed the tall grass.  It didn't take long before Phyllis and Benjamin were satisfied that the painting had not been removed from the train at this point.  They gladly returned to the jeep.  The assistant yard superintendent returned them to where they had left their rental.

"I'm getting more and more convinced that the Seurat never left Chicago," moaned Phyllis.

Benjamin frowned, "So we've just been spinning our wheels this whole trip?"

Phyllis chuckled, "Yeah, but we had a good time in New York."

"I'm sure that your grandfather will be happy to hear that," laughed Benjamin.

The two returned to the airport in Middleton to catch a flight back to Chicago.  The only flights available were to Midway Airport.  It was Duck who picked them up and drove them to the office.  They quickly apprised Phillip of everything that had transpired on their trip.

Phillip listened attentively and then leaned back in his highbacked swivel chair.

"While you were gone, detective Conroy and his boys did a detailed search of the Art Institute with their security people," Phillip revealed.  "It turned up bupkis."

Phyllis and Benjamin sighed distraughtly.

"I think that the two of you should go over to the Penn Central freight depot tomorrow morning," Phillip instructed.

The two agreed.  Phillip offered to take them to dinner, but they were eager to get home.

Friday morning Phyllis and Benjamin went directly to the railroad yard.

The freight manager at the Penn Central freight terminal looked at the two detectives.

"I understand that you're investigating the disappearance of that painting that was shipped from the Institute on Friday evening," the manager sighed.

Phyllis and Benjamin nodded.

"How can I help?" the manager asked politely.

Phyllis smiled, "I understand that the painting left the Institute between one and one-thirty

Friday afternoon and it arrived at the museum in Manhattan at one-thirty Monday morning.”

The manager quickly typed on the computer keyboard that sat in front of him.

“That sounds about right to me, but let me check,” he returned.  “Yep, that is correct.”

Phyllis frowned, “It took sixty hours to make a trip that is supposed to take sixteen hours?”

“It takes the Amtrak passenger train sixteen hours, and that’s under the best conditions,” corrected the manager.  “The minimum time that it could take for freight is twenty-two hours.  However, realistically it usually takes about thirty-six hours.”

Phyllis chuckled, “But this time it took nearly twice that long.”

The freight manager chuckled slightly, “Pardon me, but what you’re not figuring is that, although the truck with the painting left the museum at around one-thirty, the train didn’t leave for New York until about eighteen hours later.”

Benjamin looked confused, “Why so long?”

The manager chuckled again, “It takes time to hump the cars around and assemble the actual consist.  These aren't toy trains that we're talking about.  It takes time to move around tens of thousands of pounds of freight.  And the train has to be assembled in a certain order.  We have to take into consideration the weight and destinations of each and every car.  And to make matters worse, the Burlington Northern freight from the west coast was six hours late.  There were dozens of cars that needed to be integrated into our eastbound that day.  It all takes time.  And of course, on the other end, they have to breakdown the train before any individual cars can be moved into new trains or delivered to docks on private spurs.  In addition, there isn't always enough yard engines available to take private cars from the yard in Hoboken to those spurs under the streets of Manhattan."

"That still leaves forty-two hours unaccounted for," accused Benjamin.

The freight manager shook his head, "I know that it sounds bad, but it isn't really.  Once a train gets that far behind schedule, things start to snowball.  For instance, the west bound trains use the same track most of the way.  Since they're running on time, it makes more sense to have the late train stop on a siding and wait for the on time trains to pass it.  If we didn't work it that way, the on time trains would fall behind schedule and then they would make other trains fall behind schedule.  If we were to let that happen, trains all across the country would become effected and we'd really have a snarled up mess.  It might even cause accidents."

"Is that why that eastbound was pulled off onto sidings so often?" wondered Phyllis.

The manager nodded, "Including that hour and forty-one minute stop outside of Harrisburg, Pennsylvania.  We hate to have a train just sitting there like that, but sometimes we just don't have any choice.  In this case it only slowed the movement by a little under three hours."

"So the train that we're concerned with got into Hoboken after thirty nine hours of actual travel?" wondered Phyllis.

"Actually, it arrived in the Hoboken yard after twenty-two hours of actual run time.  But because it was thirty-eight hours late in arriving, things were really jammed up in Hoboken.  The freight manager there made the decision to service all the on time freight first before one hundred complaints turned into three thousand complaints.  Honestly, I'd have done the same thing," the manager sighed.

"So I have to tell the insurance company that a $125 million painting was left sitting in the yard in Hoboken, New Jersey for thirty-eight hours unattended?" lamented Phyllis.

The freight manager laughed, "It wasn't exactly unattended.  The guards from Chicago were still with it and you can believe our security people take things like that very seriously.  Yeah, there was a time when freight used to just 'fall off' the back of trains in Hoboken, but that doesn't happen anymore.  Not only do we have tons of security people there, but so does the police department, and the department of transportation.  Your painting was probably better guarded at that time than it's ever been guarded.  For my money, it left the train on that Harrisburg siding.  Did you check that out?"

"We were there yesterday," offered Phyllis.  "There were no signs of a truck anywhere along that siding."

The freight manager frowned, "Maybe they didn't haul it off.  Maybe they just transferred it to another car."

The manager once again started to pound this computer keyboard.

"I'm checking to see what was on the cars nearest to the museum car, and if there were any dead heading cars," the manager explained. "Of course, the cars behind it were the work car with your guards and then the caboose with the train crew.  We can count them out.  It says here that there were no dead heads, empty cars being moved to some location, that is.  The first car ahead of yours was a flat car with a trailer, like the ones that make up fourteen wheelers when they are hitched behind a tractor."

He continued to type.

"That trailer belongs to *Yellow* freight hauling. It was a load of books from *Lakeside Publishing* bound for their New England distribution center outside of Boston.  It was offloaded and hitched to a tractor to complete its trip on surface streets," the manager paused for an instant.  "And the receiver signed for it Tuesday morning.  I doubt that the painting was among that shipment of books, unless the guy in Boston was in on it."

"What else do you have?" asked Benjamin.

The manager returned to his typing, "The next two cars were tankers belonging to U. S. Chemical, then we have a refrigerated box car belonging to *Patrick Cudahy Meat Packing* and another belonging to *Oscar F. Mayer Company*. Next come three gondola cars of scrap iron, two flat cars loaded with steel and five boxcars containing various *Proctor and Gamble* products…"

"That's enough," interrupted Phyllis. "We've been to that siding. The terrain is pretty rugged, it's unlikely that four fat old museum guards could have carried the painting any farther than that."

The manager shrugged, "Sorry that I couldn't be any help."

"That's alright, you've been more than patient with us," offered Phyllis. "And by excluding things, we're closer to what really happened."

Benjamin and Phyllis left the Penn Central freight yard and drove across the Chicago Loop to its east side nearest to the lake. After spending an inordinate amount of time looking for a parking garage that wasn't full, the two finally walked down Michigan Avenue toward the Art Institute.

"It would have been quicker to take a cab from the freight yard and back again than to try to find parking here," complained Benjamin. "That's one thing about L A, there's always parking lots everywhere."

"And you'll go broke using them," countered Phyllis.

The two finally arrived at the Art Institute.

# Chapter Eight

# Back at the Art Institute

It was only midmorning on Friday when Phyllis and Benjamin walked into the Chicago Art Institute.  They were eagerly met by the chief of security and the museum director.

"It is fortuitous that you have come today," greeted the museum director.  "We just received the ransom instructions."

The Attlees looked at the director in anticipation.

"The letter was delivered by FedEx a few moments ago," the director went on.  "It demands that we make a wire transfer of forty million dollars to a numbered Swiss bank account.  I just gave all the information to the insurance company."

"Was there any time frame given?" wondered Phyllis.

The director nodded, "It said that we had one week to comply.  After that, they said that it goes to the highest bidder."

"That's good," Phyllis sighed. "It gives us some time."

Phyllis then asked to see the area where the painting had been shipped from and also the place where it had been prepared for its trip to New York. The museum director and security chief led them through the cavernous halls of the museum toward the freight elevator. Suddenly Phyllis stopped short.

"We were here Saturday, and I don't remember this being here," Phyllis pointed out, looking at a new display.

"That's because it wasn't here until Tuesday morning," concurred the director.

"This display was built here since Saturday?" questioned Benjamin.

"Oh, no," laughed the director. "We build our temporary displays down in the basement. Then during the night, they are moved to the place where they will be used."

The display that they were looking at was made up of three walls. They were configured in such a way that they would have looked like the letter "H" if observed from above. The center wall was more than twice as long as the two side walls.

"How big would you say that center wall is?" Phyllis asked Benjamin.

"Definitely eight foot tall and around ten feet wide," estimated Benjamin.

"You have a good eye, Professor Attlee," concurred the director. "It is eight foot tall and twelve feet wide."

"I have a feel for those dimensions," laughed Benjamin. "It's about the size of my office."

Phyllis glared at her husband.

"Will we get to see the place where this was built?" asked Phyllis.

The director said that it was exactly one of the places where they would be going. The four continued on to a deserted wing of the first floor, near where the business offices were located. The security chief opened the huge, fifteen foot wide, ten foot tall door to the freight elevator and the four rode it down to the basement. As the four stepped off the elevator, Phyllis and Benjamin looked around, taking in everything.

"Where was that display built?" asked Phyllis.

The director nodded, "The work area is down here.  I'll take you to the dock first and then you can see the carpenters' work area."

The director led them past dozens of crates holding priceless works of art.  There were paintings leaning against crates and walls.  There were statues with canvas tarps over them.  There were also dozens of empty frames.  It was truly amazing to see what was not on permanent display.  The director led the Attlees back to a pair of enormous swing open doors.

"This leads to the dock," announced the director as the security chief unlocked the doors.

"No alarm, or is it just turned off right now?" wondered Benjamin.

"No real reason to have an alarm here," returned the chief of security, "There are cameras on the freight elevator, and an alarm on the roll up doors on the dock."

"So, basically, once you're down here, you have the run of the place," stated Phyllis.

The two museum employees nodded.

"But you need to have a key to open the door to the elevator and even the stairs need a key to be accessed," added the chief of security.

"Who has access to the basement?" inquired Benjamin.

"Just about everyone," replied the director.

"The carpenters, the warehouse people, the receiver, and, in addition, of course, the cleaning staff keep all their supplies down here," offered the security Chief.

"And also the security personnel have access," added the director.

Phyllis and Benjamin nodded as they stepped out into the loading dock area.  Yes, indeed, there was a large roll down steel door with an electronic alarm system on it and cameras aimed at it.  Phyllis and Benjamin were satisfied.  The director then escorted them to the work area.

"This is where the carpenters work most of the time," advised the director.

"Of course, they also do remodeling and repair work throughout the museum," added the security chief.  "That's where they are right now."

"So those big walls were constructed here and then moved to where they are now?" asked Phyllis.

"Yes," affirmed the director. "The crew worked all weekend."

"They worked all this weekend?" exclaimed Phyllis.

"I know what you're thinking," chuckled the security chief. "There's no way they could have gotten that seven by ten foot painting out of here without being seen by the security cameras upstairs."

"The painting was gone by that time anyway," reminded the director.

"Were they the ones who crated the painting?" inquired Benjamin.

"The painting was brought down here Tuesday night right after closing. Then on Wednesday our restoration and repair team covered it with the protective wrapping," the director explained. "Then Wednesday and Thursday our carpentry crew custom built the crate. We shipped it on Friday."

"Did the carpentry crew spend time alone with the painting?" asked Phyllis.

"I suppose so, but like the chief said there's no way that it could have been removed from the basement without being seen," objected the director.

"Those walls of that display that we saw upstairs are pretty big," Benjamin said casually. "How on earth do you move them?"

The security chief chuckled, "With great difficulty.  The carpenters and a few cleaning people put them on pallet jacks in three separate pieces."

"That's why we do it at night.  It would be much too problematic to do that while visitors are in the museum, not to mention the liability issue," agreed the director.  "Once they have the temporary displays in position, they assemble the panels and do a little touchup with spackle and paint.  Then it's our display dressers that position the art work."

"So, this is really a big operation," sighed Benjamin.  "And there are a lot of people involved."

The director nodded, "Too many to keep any kind of unlawful activities quiet."

The director then led them to the south side of the basement.  The first thing that became immediately obvious was that this part of the basement was cleaner with freshly painted walls and a finished ceiling with no exposed beams.  There was a wall with large windows in it at the far end of the basement.  This part of the basement was also well lit, much more so than the areas they had just covered.

"This is the restoration room," announced the director.  "This is where our experts clean and restore the works of art."

The party stopped and looked through the large picture windows.  More than a dozen people worked on various pieces of priceless art.

"We usually only allow employees in this area," said the director.  "But we can make an exception in your case."

Phyllis smiled, "Are there any rooms coming off this one?" asked Phyllis.

"Nope," returned the chief of security.  "There is not even a closet.  What you see is what you get."

"Yes, you can see it all from here," agreed the director.

"Then I don't think that we'll be needing to go in," returned Phyllis.

"And that pretty much ends our tour of the unseen portions of our museum," offered the director.

"The Chicago police had men searching every inch of this basement since we reported the theft," reported the chief of security.

"Did they find any thing that was unusual?" asked Benjamin.

"Well, they certainly didn't find the Seurat!" exclaimed the director.

Benjamin chuckled, "No, I mean anything out of place, or something that shouldn't have been here at all, or maybe something that had been moved around for no reason."

Both men thought carefully and then shook their heads.

"I didn't expect so, but I needed to ask," returned Benjamin.

"Do you ever have any of the general public come down here?" asked Phyllis.

The director shrugged, "Not really the general public, but we do have several member events when we have a tour for those who want to see it."

"And twice a year we have tours for the students of the school of the Art Institute," reminded the chief of security.

"Do many of the members take advantage of that tour?" wondered Benjamin.

The director chuckled, "No, not very many. Most of them are too interested in the free booze and food upstairs."

"And also, the models and artists that are in attendance," snickered the security chief.

"I do have to say that the students do take a greater interest in this area," admitted the director.

"I would have when I was in college," agreed Benjamin. "It is fascinating, with a definite mystique about it."

"Oh, yes, there are all sorts of strange and weird stories about the basement," laughed the director. "You could write a book about the legends concerning it. Perhaps your friend, Doctor Weatherby, will one day, Professor Attlee."

"You never know, Henry's always looking for a good story," chuckled Benjamin.

"And a quick buck," added Phyllis.

The director chuckled, "Well, if he ever does, we would be more than happy to publish it and sell it in our museum store. You see, we don't mind making a quick buck either. With tales of the eerie environment sprinkled in, along with some tall tales about ghosts and apparitions, and not to mention the true stories about thefts and daring recoveries, like you and the Stars of Bethlehem, the students and tourists would eat it up."

"I'll have to mention it to my uncle," chuckled Phyllis.

"The heck with Henry," snickered Benjamin. "Maybe I should do it!"

Everyone laughed as they headed back toward the first floor.

"Would you like to take a look at the security tapes from the weekend?" offered the security chief.

"No," smiled Phyllis. "You have good people working here."

"But, just to be on the safe side, we should have copies of your employee records," added Benjamin.

"We figured that you would, so we already made copies for you," returned the director. "And seriously, Professor, should you take the idea to heart and actually write a book about our weird basement, I bet it would sell.  Such a book by a respected professor, who is also a private detective and one of those responsible for finding the devil's scepter, would be an instant hit.  We would make sure that all the guides would mention it on all the tours."

Benjamin smiled, "I'll give it some thought."

After receiving the files, Phyllis and Benjamin returned to their office.

"It's going to take a ton of time to go over these files," Benjamin complained.

Phyllis shook her head, "We only need to look at those carpenters."

"I thought that you were zeroing in on them. But the problem is how they got the thing out," Benjamin said.

"If they got the painting out," returned Phyllis.

"True, they would only need to get it out if they were going to sell it," agreed Benjamin.  "This is being held for ransom."

"That warehouse area of the basement is cavernous.  They could have switched out the painting while they were building the crate and hidden it somewhere in that mass of crates and boxes," moaned Phyllis.

"Conroy has had a squad of officers searching for it for a week now, with no success," complained Benjamin.

"I bet that half of those guys didn't even know what they were looking for," Phyllis sighed. "And there has got to be secret rooms and passages down there that only long time employees know about."

"So you figure on someone that's been around for a while?" wondered Benjamin.

Phyllis sighed, "It could have been almost anyone, but my money is on the carpenters. They spend the most time down there.  And it seems like they pretty much have the run of the place, not to mention the fact that they all have tools with them all the time without anyone ever being suspicious.  Let's get their phone records and see if any of them have been making any calls to Switzerland."

Benjamin shuffled through the files for a few seconds finding the carpenter crew files.

"Gus Zimmer, George Sanchez, and Sammy McDonald," Benjamin read. "I'll get over to the phone company and check them out. If we had a computer terminal, I could do it from here in seconds."

"Someday," snickered Phyllis. "But it will probably be on the same day that you see pigs flying."

Benjamin laughed and then left for the telephone company offices. Phyllis went into her grandfather's office to inform him of what was going on.

"I heard about the ransom instructions," Phillip moaned. "I told them to hold off as long as they could. You better have something."

Phyllis told him that they had a good lead.

It was after six in the evening when Benjamin returned from his mission. Both Phyllis and Phillip were waiting anxiously for him.

"Who was it?" Phyllis pressed excitedly.

Benjamin smiled, "Sammy McDonald made several calls to Zurich Switzerland in the last month."

"McDonald!" exclaimed Phillip as he handed Phyllis a twenty dollar bill. "I bet on Zimmer."

"The calls were made from McDonald's phone, but I'd bet that it was Zimmer doing the talking," insisted Benjamin.

"Why do you say that?" wondered Phillip.

"I remembered that Brother Volker was with Interpol," replied Benjamin. "So, I called him from the phone company office. That's why I'm so late. He said that he'd get right back to me. So I waited for his call. When he did call back he said that the number belongs to a Karl Zimmer."

"That sure clouds our little bet, Sweetheart," snickered Phillip.

"The bet was on who's phone was used, not who did the talking," laughed Phyllis.

"It's not like you need the twenty," groaned Phillip.

"Tell you what," Phyllis sighed. "I'll buy dinner at the Golden Phoenix."

The three adjourned to the Chinese restaurant down the block.

# Chapter Eight

# Egg Rolls and Plaster Walls

As the three detectives sat eating their dinner special for three, Phyllis couldn't help but think about the Art Institute. Something bothered her.

"I can't get that new display wall out of my mind," Phyllis sighed.

"What display?" wondered Phillip.

"There's a new display of art by some Hawaiian artist that I've never heard of on the first floor," explained Benjamin. "It wasn't there when we visited on Saturday."

"What about it?" considered Phillip.

"The center wall of the display is twelve feet wide and eight feet tall," Phyllis returned.

"Yep, they built the thing in the basement in three pieces and then carried each piece up to the first floor. Once they had it all there, they put it all together," added Benjamin. "It must have been a real pain in the butt!"

Phillip snickered, "And you think that the Sunday afternoon thingamabob is inside that wall, Sweetheart?"

Phyllis nodded.

"That's pretty unlikely," refuted Phillip.

Phyllis looked at her grandfather with concern.

Phillip chuckled, "You don't understand.  That wall ain't empty inside."

Phyllis now looked confused.

"You see, the wall is made up of two long studs, two by fours, twelve feet long on the top and bottom.  Then there's two eight footers, one on each end.  But that only makes up the frame of the thing.  Inside there's another two by four stud every sixteen inches.  And the whole thing is covered with plasterboard."

Phyllis crinkled her forehead, "What if you didn't have the studs inside?"

Both Phillip and Benjamin laughed.  Phyllis looked angrily at them.

"Excuse me for not knowing anything about building walls," complained Phyllis.  "After all, as everyone always forgets, I am a girl."

Both of the guys looked contrite.

"I've never forgotten that you're a girl, and a pretty great one at that," confessed Benjamin.

Phyllis smiled at her husband.

"Stop being such a… a… a husband, Ben!" complained Phillip.

"Without the studs inside, the entire thing would be extremely weak.  In fact, the seams of the plasterboards wouldn't lineup evenly and would probably flex in and out.  They might even crack," explained Benjamin.

"You'd never be able to hang anything on the wall.  If you leaned on it, the plasterboard would break," added Phillip.

Phyllis frowned, "I suppose that there's no way that the painting could be inside that wall."

Phillip and Benjamin shook their heads, but then Benjamin stopped as a strange expression swept across his face.

"Unless…" Benjamin sighed softly.

Phyllis perked up, "Unless what?"

Benjamin looked intently at Phillip, "What if, instead of two by fours, they used two by sixes to construct the outside frame?  Then they could just reinforce it with two by twos every sixteen inches on the inside."

"And if they placed two of the two by twos at each sixteen inch support point aligned with the facings of the two by sixes, the plasterboard would be even and strong enough for what it's being used for," continued Phillip.

Benjamin smiled, "And there would be a two inch space between every two by two."

"And since there are walls on both sides of the one in question, at ninety degree angles to it, no one would ever notice that the wall was thicker than it should be," Phillip agreed.

Phyllis glanced quickly between the two, "Does, whatever the two of you just said, mean that they could hide the painting between the two by twos?"

"Absolutely!" returned the two simultaneously.

All three detectives grinned with delight.

"It's perfect, the darn thing is perfectly safe inside the Art Institute," laughed Phillip.  "First thing in the morning we gotta call Sean and tell him all of this.  He's gonna want Detective Conroy and some uniforms at the museum tomorrow about the time that the two of you get over there to make a few holes in that wall."

It was nearly noon Friday, September 5th, when Phyllis and Benjamin met Detective Frank Conroy and his new partner, Detective Bob Matthews, and six uniformed police officers at the Chicago Art Institute.  A very concerned looking museum director greeted them along with a determined looking security chief.

"I take it that you have some disturbing news for me?" asked the museum director.

Phyllis smiled, "Not so disturbing as you might think."

"Then why all the police?" returned the director.

"I hope that we'll be making an arrest today," Phyllis advised.

"An arrest here?" groaned the security chief. "That means that you must believe that one of our employees stole the painting."

Phyllis nodded her head.

"That's not exactly good news," moaned the director.

"The good news is that the painting never left the Institute," interjected Benjamin.

The security chief looked inquisitively at Detective Conroy.

"Don't look at me, I'm just along for the ride," Conroy snickered.

"That's impossible," protested the director. "We've been searching every inch of the Institute since it disappeared. If it were here we'd certainly have found it."

"I hate to disagree with you Mrs. Attlee," lamented the security chief. "However, it's true. We've left no rock unturned."

"It's not under a rock," countered Phyllis.

"It's inside a rock," added Benjamin. "Sheet rock to be exact."

Everyone looked confused as Phyllis led the group through the museum to where the display of the painting from the unknown Hawaiian artist was hung.

"I hate to tell you this, but my husband is going to have to make a hole in your nice new wall," announced Phyllis.

"You think that it's inside this wall?" exclaimed the director. "That's absolutely impossible."

Benjamin took a screwdriver from his pocket and pressed it against the plasterboard.

"What do you think that you're doing?" screamed the director, grabbing at Benjamin's hand.

"Let him go," instructed Frank Conroy.

Benjamin scraped and scratched at the plasterboard until he made a circular depression in it.  He then carefully breached the backing paper of the plasterboard and pulled the circular piece away, revealing a six inch diameter hole in the wall.  Detective Matthews shined a flashlight into the hole.

"Son of a gun!" exclaimed Matthews.  "There's a picture in here."

"Not a picture," corrected Phyllis.  "It's a painting, Georges Seurat's *Sunday Afternoon on the Island of Grand Jatte,* to be exact."

The director and the security chief stood dumbfounded at the revelation.

"And where can I find the carpenters?" inquired Detective Frank Conroy.

"I'll take you to them," offered the chief of security.

The director quickly called for some of the cleaning crew and art restoration staff to come and remove the rest of the wall.

As Conroy and Matthews collected Zimmer, McDonald, and Sanchez, museum workers removed the unknown Hawaiian artist's paintings and carefully took apart the temporary display wall.  Benjamin had been correct.  The wall was framed with two by sixes.  There were, indeed, two two by twos every sixteen inches for the support.  The museum workers did their demolition very slowly and cautiously.  Phyllis and Benjamin waited until the job was complete before leaving for the 18th precinct.

By the time that the Attlees arrived at the station house, the three carpenters had already been fingerprinted and processed for booking.  The three carpenters were each seated in a different interrogation room awaiting Lieutenant Flynn.  Since the painting was now officially recovered, Clark Investigations no longer had any interest in the case.  The prosecution of those who had stolen it for ransom was a matter concerning the police.  Even though this was true, the Attlees were welcome to watch the interrogations.

Lieutenant Flynn first spoke with Zimmer, as he figured that it was he that was the mastermind behind the heist.  Zimmer was totally uncooperative, only saying that he wouldn't say anything without a lawyer present.  The public defender was called for Zimmer, as Lieutenant Flynn moved on to McDonald.

McDonald denied having any knowledge of how the Seurat painting could have gotten into the false wall.

"You have no way of proving that we had anything to do with it," McDonald laughed.

Lieutenant Flynn stopped to talk briefly with Phyllis and Benjamin before he went into interrogate Sanchez.

"I don't know that we're going to have a strong enough case against these guys for the district attorney to take into court without some other evidence than the fact that they were alone with the painting," Flynn complained.  "All we got is a phone call to Zurich on McDonald's phone. That aint a heck of a lot to go into court with. We've got evidence technicians going over that Seurat with a fine toothed comb and so far we got nada."

Phyllis shrugged, "Sorry Jack, I doubt that there'll be any fingerprints or other evidence on the painting.  These guys were just too smart for that."

Jack Flynn shook his head and sighed, "Well at least you'll get your finder's fee, if nothing else."

Disheartened, Flynn stepped into the last interrogation room.  George Sanchez sat quietly, sweating nervously in the room. Lieutenant Flynn pulled out his chair on the opposite side of the table from Sanchez.  Flynn looked intently at the fidgeting and obviously frightened man.  Sanchez would not make eye contact with Flynn.  The lieutenant sat staring silently at the man while he considered his approach.  Flynn wondered if there wasn't more hanging over Sanchez's head than just a prison sentence.

Flynn decided to take a shot, "Where are you from, Sanchez?"

The man lowered his head and nearly broke into tears.

"You're not Puerto Rican, you're Cuban?" asked Flynn.

Sanchez began sobbing.

"That's what I figured," Flynn said softly. "You ain't going to jail for this, you're going back to Cuba.  Yeah, Fidel's gonna just love to get you back, isn't he?"

Sanchez didn't answer, he just sat and cried pitifully.

"You know what?" sighed Flynn.  "I don't want you to have to go back any more than you do."

Suddenly Sanchez turned his eyes up toward the police officer.

"You know what I think?" Flynn said softly and slowly, "I think that you didn't want to have anything to do with this thing.  Why would you?"  You got a good job, probably the best that you've ever had.  Why would you risk going back to Cuba and life in prison, or maybe death in prison."

Sanchez stopped sobbing and looked at Flynn in anticipation.

Flynn smiled, "I think that Zimmer forced you to get into this deal.  He said that he would turn you into immigration if you didn't help him.  I bet that he didn't even offer you any of the money, did he?"

Sanchez shook his head, "He said that he would tell on me and my family if I didn't help them."

"You know what?" Flynn sighed.  "We have something in this country called political asylum for people like you, good hard working people, who escape from places like Cuba."

Sanchez looked surprised and interested.

"Yeah, even though you came here illegally, you can get to stay because you would be in extreme danger if you went home," Flynn explained. "I could help you get asylum."

Sanchez perked up, "You can do that for me?"

"Sure," Flynn offered. "But, not if you're a criminal."

Once again Sanchez lowered his head, "Then it is too late for me, Señor."

"Maybe not," Flynn countered. "If you were to help me, I could tell the I.N.S. that you had been cooperative and that because of you two felons were put away. If that were so, I know that they would be inclined to keep you and yours away from Fidel."

Sanchez nodded his head enthusiastically, "I'll do anything to help you, Señor."

Lieutenant Flynn smiled with satisfaction and leaned back in his chair, "Tell me how it all started."

Sanchez breathed heavily, "One day about four months ago the Director of the Institute came down to our work place in the basement. He goes to Señor Gus and tells him that the painting with all the dots is going to go to someplace in New York for a few months. A week later he tells Gus that we will have to build a display for some paintings. I think that this gets Señor Gus thinking. So one day I see Gus and Sammy talking in the back of the basement. They are looking at me…how you say?… like, 'forastero', someone that does not belong."

"An outsider," offered Lieutenant Flynn. "An outsider, someone that they don't trust."

"Si! No confiable," Sanchez nodded. "The next day Señor Sammy comes and tells me that they want me to help them to take the dot painting and if I don't, they will tell immigration services about how me and my familia come to America on small boat from Cuba. I am so scared. I say 'yes', I help them. I do anything to stay here."

Flynn nodded, "Of course. So who's idea was it to hide it inside the display wall?"

"Señor Gus," Sanchez returned. "It was he who think about how to make it fit inside. The porteros, cleaning hombres, and the people who make reparar bring the dot painting down to workroom. They envolver, wrap up, the dot panting and then leave it by us to make the caja de carton. Gus and Sammy already made the falso lienzo, so when no one was there we just switched it. We take the envase off the dot painting and cover the falso lienzo with it. We put the real painting inside the wall and covered it with the placas de yeso. Then we put the falso lienzo inside the caja to ship. That is all I know."

Flynn exhaled hard, "My Spanish is worse than your English. But, what I think you said was that after the thing was wrapped up, you guys were left alone to make the crate."

"Si," nodded Sanchez.

"And then you switched a fake canvas for the real one, putting the fake inside the crate and the real one inside the wall?" Flynn asked.

Once again Sanchez nodded eagerly, "Si."

"And if I get a guy to write all this down, you will be willing to sign it and swear to God that it's the truth?" asked Flynn.

Sanchez smiled broadly, "Si, jurar por Dios! Si!"

Lieutenant Flynn smiled a broadly as Sanchez.

"He got them," exclaimed Phyllis. "Zimmer and McDonald are going up the river."

"Our deal for the recovery is one percent, right?" asked Benjamin.  "One and a quarter million dollars."

Phyllis frowned, "One percent of the ransom demand, not the value of the painting.  It would have to have been taken to be fenced, for us to get one percent of the total value.  It's still four hundred thousand dollars."

"Phillip was right, we could buy a dozen computers for that much," sighed Benjamin.

Phyllis looked at her husband sympathetically, "Oh you poor trusting soul.  You should know by now that my grandfather hates to spend money, and he hates change even more.  And the thing that he hates the most is technology."

"But he likes being the best!" Benjamin countered.  "And being the first agency in town, probably in the country, with a state of the art computer system linked to the police and the FBI National Crime Information Center, has really got to score points with the high price clients.  I bet that every insurance company in the country will be impressed with us."

"I found the *Stars of Bethlehem*, the *Emerald Isle*, the *Dachimer Blue,* and I just recovered the $125,000,000.00 *Sunday Afternoon on the*

*Island of Grand Jatte.* Every insurance company in the country is already impressed." Phyllis laughed.

Benjamin sighed, "Maybe I should just use the computer to write my book about the ghosts of the Art Institute."

"Oh right!  Gramps is really going to fork out forty grand so you can write a book on agency time," Phyllis snickered.  "It took me five years to get him to buy air conditioners!"

Benjamin frowned.

"You got a better chance of him buying an expensive cappuccino and expresso machine," laughed Phyllis.  "At least he likes a good cup of joe."

"And Alice would be just as lost operating one of them as a computer," chuckled Benjamin.

"Oh, she'd be even more lost on the coffee machines," snickered Phyllis.

The two returned to the office to inform Phillip of the closing of another case!  And then they would all be off to celebrate!